PATRICIA SCANLAN

Second Chance

POOLBEG

This book was commissioned by
Finglas Adult Reading & Writing Scheme
and
City of Dublin Vocational Education Committee

Sponsorship was provided by C.D.V.E.C.
Adult Education Board for printing of
Second Chance

Acknowledgements:

Thanks to Alil O'Shaughnessy of Finglas Library
and Frances McManus of the Finglas Adult
Reading & Writing Scheme,
Coláiste Eoin

Published 1996 by
Poolbeg Press Ltd,
123 Baldoyle Industrial Estate,
Dublin 13, Ireland

A catalogue record for this book is available from the British Library.

ISBN 1 85371 695 2

Illustrations by Laura Cronin
Cover design by Poolbeg Group Services Ltd
Set by Poolbeg Group Services Ltd in Times
Printed ColourBooks Ltd

Chapter One

"I'm going." Tony O'Neill gave the door a good slam.

"And don't bother coming back," his wife Jean shouted angrily. Tony heard the baby start to cry. He wanted to go back into the house and cuddle her but Jean would say he was spoiling her. Tony looked back. He could see his mother-in-law peering through the lace curtains that hung on the windows of her small redbrick house. When she saw him looking back she hastily dropped the curtains. Tony sighed. Mrs Feeny would blame him for the row. His mother-in-law blamed him for everything these days.

Tony walked slowly in the direction of Phibsboro. It was starting to rain. The sky was low and grey. Big raindrops plopped onto the ground in front of him. That was all he needed. He quickened his pace. He could take shelter in the newsagents down the road. The rain came faster and heavier until it was a downpour. Tony had to run the last few steps to shelter.

He stood looking at the newspapers in the rack, his eyes skimming across the headlines. Interest rates up. Mortgages up. Unemployment figures up. The punt down. All bad news. As usual. He knew all about bad news. Being unemployed and living with your mother-in-law was about the worst thing.

He'd been a printer in a small printing firm. It had specialised mostly in wedding stationery and Thank You cards and party invitations and such like. The firm had been doing well. Then there had been a postal strike. Orders stopped coming in. Existing orders had not been paid for. The staff began to get very worried. With good reason. After several weeks, with no sign of a settlement in sight, the boss called a meeting. The business had failed and he had no choice but to make his staff redundant.

That was the worst day of Tony's life. Going

home to their flat to tell Jean the news had been dreadful. He felt that he had let her down terribly. After all it was his duty to provide for his wife and new baby daughter. Some of his mates were redundant and he had never been able to understand their misery at signing on the dole. He couldn't understand when they talked about it taking away their pride. Wasn't it great to get money handed out to you? You could spend all day doing exactly what you wanted to do, he once joked with Mick, a pal of his.

"It's not like that at all," Mick snapped.

Tony thought he was being a bit touchy. Now he understood. Signing on robbed a man of his pride. Robbed him of his independence. And robbed him of his will to get up off his ass and do something.

The first morning he had signed on he felt worthless. Although the girl behind the counter had been very nice and helpful, Tony went home to Jean, put the money on the table, and cried like a baby. His wife tried to comfort him. It was only temporary. Things would improve. He would get another job, she assured him.

Nothing she said eased his fears. Tony had

seen men like himself, men younger than him, and older men who had been signing on for years. They too had tried to get jobs. And failed, time and again. Why should he be any different? New technology that made man's skills unnecessary was helping to cut down on the workforce. Computers didn't take tea and lunch-breaks. They didn't take an hour off each week to cash a pay-cheque. They didn't need unions to fight for their rights. Bloody computers, he hated them.

That first terrible week of his unemployment he sat down with the Golden Pages directory and wrote to every printing firm listed. He wrote to all the newspapers, local and national. Jean, who had worked as a typist before her marriage, typed his CV neatly and expertly. He wrote over fifty letters seeking employment. He cycled the length and breadth of the city hand-delivering them. He prayed that the postal dispute would end so that the postman could start delivering the replies. Surely, out of the fifty firms he had written to, he'd get a job offer from one of them.

With great anticipation Tony heard the ending

of the postal dispute announced on the six o'clock news one evening several weeks later. The next morning he was waiting for the postman. To his dismay all he got were several brown envelopes containing bills, and a card from his sister who had been in Spain on holidays.

"Don't worry," Jean assured him. "They'll have lots of mail to sort, there's probably loads of replies waiting for you."

Tony got two replies out of the fifty letters he had sent out. Both regretting that they could not offer him employment. He was gutted. Despair enveloped him. What a failure he was as a husband and a father. "Stop worrying, we're managing all right. Something will turn up," Jean encouraged. But he could see the new worry lines in her face. The anxious furrowing of her brow when more brown envelopes with their unwelcome bills dropped on the doormat in the mornings.

"Maybe I should go to England," Tony suggested glumly. "I'd surely get a job there."

"It's as bad there as it is here. Hold on for a while, We're not on our uppers yet," his wife said, but Tony could not get rid of the nagging anxiety that weighed him down. ●

They quickly learned to economise. No more Chinese take-aways. No newspapers. No more biscuits or cakes. They started to buy cheaper loo rolls and cheaper nappies for the baby. Yellow pack labels saved them a few pounds. As fast as the sand in an egg-timer, their little nest egg of savings disappeared. Jean suggested that maybe they should start looking for a less expensive flat.

Her mother stepped in and suggested that they come and live with her until things picked up and her son-in-law got another job.

"I think it's for the best, Tony. At least it won't be taking an enormous amount out of your dole money in rent. I could look after baby Angela for Jean if she was able to get a part-time job," Mrs Feeny said with that delicate breathy voice that hid a will of iron. Tony knew he would be making a big mistake by agreeing to his mother-in-law's suggestion. They'd manage on their own. Thousands . . . no millions of people managed in similar circumstances and he'd get a job somewhere, he knew it. "Let's wait another little while," he urged his wife. But he could see that she wanted to move in with her mother.

"I'll get a job in an office or maybe a shop or a café for a couple of hours a day. Mam can mind Angela. She'd love it and it would give us a few extra bob," Jean pleaded the day they gave back their video and stopped their Cablelink payments. Then the washing-machine broke down and Tony just didn't have the money to get it repaired. Jean started bringing the washing around to her mother's. She spent longer and longer there. In the end, Tony agreed to go and live in the redbrick house off the North Circular Road. He had never felt so fed up in his life.

Now, nearly a year later, he was sick to death of his life. Sick to death of his mother-in-law and, right at this minute, sick to death of his wife. Especially after their row this morning. He stared glumly out of the shop window. The rain was easing off. Where was he going to go today anyway? He had no destination in mind when he had barged out of the house earlier on. All he wanted to do then was to get away from

his wife and her mother⁄ He put his hand in his
trouser pocket and took out the loose coins that
jangled there. One pound and thirty pence, he
counted, hardly a fortune, still it was better than
nothing. Last week he'd only had twenty pence
left on his dole day. He wouldn't mind buying a
paper and going for a cup of coffee and a read.
But if he bought a paper he wouldn't have
enough to buy anything to eat later on. He had
better stay out of Jean's hair for the rest of the
day. Tony sighed. He put the coins back in his
pocket and headed up towards Phibsboro.

Chapter Two

Jean scraped a slice of burnt toast. She had burnt her breakfast because of *him*. She was very angry. Just who did Tony think he was? You'd think he'd be a bit grateful to her mother for taking them in. For helping out when they were stuck. And they were stuck. Beggars couldn't be choosers. Her mother's generosity had eased their financial situation a lot. Why couldn't Tony be more gracious?

Jean sat down. She took a bite of toast. She made a face. It tasted horrible. Tony hadn't had any breakfast either. Jean felt a pang. She was feeling remorseful now that her burst of temper was spent. She shouldn't have shouted at him the way she had. Just because he let the milk boil over. Her mother had started moaning about the way milk stains the cooker. There had been a full-scale row.

Her mother was not easy to live with. Jean had to admit it. She was fussy. She liked everything just so. If Tony left a paper on the chair she'd fold it up neatly and put it in the paper-rack. Always with a little arch of the eyebrows and eyes thrown up to heaven. Bridie Feeny never had to speak to make her disapproval known. One arch of her plucked eyebrows was enough.

Angela whimpered in her high-chair. Jean stood up and gently lifted her out.

"Poor baba," she soothed. Angela snuggled in for a cuddle. Jean gave a little smile. They had been so excited when she'd found out she was going to have a baby. Together they had decorated the small room in the flat. They had bought nursery wallpaper. She had even got a border to match. It was a beautiful border. It had little cows jumping over the moon.

Jean felt sadness well up. How she would love to be back in her cosy little flat. Just the three of them. Everything had been going so well for them. They had been saving for a mortgage. Their dream of buying their own house was shattered now. All their savings were gone. Tony felt a terrible failure. He felt he had let her and Angela down. Jean sighed. He shouldn't blame himself. It wasn't his fault. He was a good husband. And she loved him.

"Maamaa," Angela interrupted her musings. Jean looked down at the little curly fair head. Tenderly she kissed her daughter. Angela was starting to talk. It was fascinating to listen to the garbled sounds and try and make sense of them. She could say hot. Everything was "hot". Jean had to watch her like a hawk now that she was crawling. Angela was fascinated by the fire. But fortunately "aha hot" was enough to stop her in her tracks. She'd be one in a couple of weeks. It was hard to believe.

Gently she laid her daughter on the floor. She watched her scoot around. Propelling herself on her little arms and legs.

Jean cleared the dirty dishes off the table. She filled the sink with hot soapy water. She washed the dishes slowly. Where had Tony gone she wondered?

Jean stared out the window into the small back garden. Her mother kept it immaculate. But, despite Bridie's best efforts, autumn leaves covered the neat lawn like a patchwork quilt.

Jean watched the early morning sun shining on the damson trees. There had been a shower when Tony left. It was over now. The sun was emerging from behind the grey clouds. She could see patches of blue in the sky. It was early autumn. Their leaves were still crisp on the branches. Gold, red, russet, brown and some still green. The slanting rays of the sun danced over them. The light breeze made them tremble on the branches. A little gust now and then would make them quiver and rustle. And then some would float lightly down to join the crisp crunchy pile beneath the tree.

It was a mild autumn so far. The rambling pink rose was still in bloom. So were the fuchsias in her mother's hanging baskets. Their full pink-and-white blooms were glorious against the whitewashed walls. Tubs of pink and red geraniums dotted the yard. Jean loved to sit out there on a sunny afternoon with Angela. It was a little haven of peace.

"Would you look at those leaves," Bridie Feeny said crossly. She came and stood beside her daughter. She picked up the tea towel and started to dry up. "I think they look pretty," Jean reflected.

"Pretty!" exclaimed her mother. "They're a nuisance. They're so untidy. I cleared that garden two days ago. There wasn't a leaf to be seen. And now look at the place. I'm going to get those damson trees cut down."

Jean threw her eyes up to heaven. Her mother made the same threat every year. But then spring would come. Each year white frothy blossoms would burst from the young buds. It was a glorious sight. Then the green leaves would appear. Later, as spring turned to summer, the damsons started to grow fat and juicy. They looked like big purple grapes.

After a long hot summer the branches would bow under the weight of their fruit. Jean and Bridie would spend an afternoon picking them. Then Bridie would make pots of dark sweet damson jam. The memory of fresh Vienna roll, spread thick with butter and topped with the tasty jam made Jean's mouth water.

The last few years had not produced a good crop. The summers had been cool and cloudy. This year there hadn't been enough damsons to make jam.

"What are you going to do with yourself today?" Bridie asked. She reached down and lifted her granddaughter into her arms. Angela squirmed. She wanted to keep on exploring. "This one is getting a mind of her own," Bridie said tartly. "Just like her father!"

"Don't start!" Jean warned. "I've had enough for one morning."

Bridie glared at her daughter. "You've had enough! *You've* had enough. What about me? Just because I didn't want my cooker ruined with hot spilt milk. That Tony has a sharp tongue." She sniffed.

"Mother, do you want us to move out?" Jean demanded.

"Don't talk nonsense," Bridie retorted. "Where would you go?"

"We'd get a flat from the Corporation," Jean snapped.

"There's no need for that kind of talk," Bridie said hastily.

15

"There is need," Jean fumed. She dried her hands. "I'm going to get dressed. I'm going in to the Housing Department to ask them to put us on the list. Then we'll be out from under your feet. Tony was right. I should never have let you persuade me to come home." She felt the tears come to her eyes. She hurried out of the kitchen not wanting her mother to see them.

Jean ran upstairs into her small back bedroom. She flung herself on the bed. Tears slid down her cheeks. She didn't think she could stand much more. She had said that she was going to see about getting on the housing list. Maybe she should do it. Things couldn't go on as they were. Jean sat up and wiped her eyes. It was her children's allowance day today. She would call into the post office to collect it. Then she would get the bus into town. She must check the address of the Housing Department. She wasn't too sure if they had moved to the new civic offices. She hoped they hadn't. The civic offices were not that handy to get to. Jervis Street was much more convenient.

Jean went to the small wardrobe that held all their clothes. She took out her good black ski pants. She wanted to look smart. It helped, when you were down in the dumps. She chose her favourite pink cashmere jumper to go with the pants. Swiftly she began to dress. Enough was enough. It was time to do something about their situation.

Bridie put Angela back down on the floor and stood frowning at the kitchen sink. Why on earth was Jean picking on *her*? Anyone would think it was her fault that Tony and Jean had problems. *She* had gone out of her way to help them. She had opened her home to them. *This* was the thanks she got. Bridie pursed her lips. She should have known better than to expect gratitude. She dried the knives and spoons and settled them neatly in the drawer. She put the butter in the fridge. She wiped the top of the marmalade dish and put it in the top press. She gave the press door a good slam because she was so annoyed. There were cornflakes all over the table mat where Tony had been sitting. He was most untidy.

She glanced at her granddaughter who was gazing wide-eyed at the clothes tumbling around in the washing-machine. Angela was her pride and joy. How lonely her life would be without her daughter and precious granddaughter. And, to tell the truth, she liked having a man in the house at night. Since they'd come to live with her, Bridie slept soundly.

When she had been on her own, she'd slept fitfully. Always listening for unusual noises. Two houses on the street had been burgled. Bridie was terrified the same would happen to her. Now that Jean and Tony were living with her she felt protected.

But it was hard getting used to having people around the house all day. She had got into a routine of her own that suited her. She liked keeping a tidy house. Tony was not a tidy person. He didn't fold up his newspapers neatly. He left his jacket hanging on the back of a chair. It drove her mad. She had asked him to hang it up in the press under the stairs. When she asked him, he would do it for a few days. Then he would forget. It was most annoying. Her dear dead husband Tom had been very neat in his habits. "A place for everything and

18

everything in its place," was his favourite saying.

Bridie's lip trembled. She missed Tom. He'd been a good husband. He was a quiet man. He let Bridie make the decisions. That suited her. Bridie was an organiser. They'd rarely had rows. Their life was a comforting routine that seldom varied. Breakfast together. Then he went to work. He worked in a furniture shop in town. She cleaned and tidied the house and did the shopping. Then she'd prepare lunch. Which was served up promptly at one o'clock. Except on Sundays. On Sundays they had lunch at one-thirty.

After lunch Tom would go back to work and Bridie would garden or knit until it was time for Tom to come home for his tea. After tea they would go up to the Phoenix Park and go for a walk if the weather was fine.

Some would say it was a dull life. But she and Tom had been happy until he'd died suddenly of a massive stroke two years ago. Now all she had was trouble and strife. When Tony was made redundant, Bridie urged Jean to persuade him to come and live with her. It was the ideal solution. She was sure of it. But it hadn't worked out as she had thought. Having three people under her feet all day was not easy. Her little routines were interrupted. She was in a state of constant tension. She worried about Angela burning herself at the fire. Or pulling the standard lamp down on top of herself.

"Ga Ga!" A small pair of hands grabbed Bridie's skirt. She looked down at her granddaughter. Angela was struggling to pull herself upright. She was almost walking now.

Bridie felt love flood through her. She leaned down and picked up the little girl. "What is it my precious?" she crooned. "Who's a lovely girl? You're my little darling." She cuddled the toddler tightly. It would be awful if Jean and Tony moved away to the outer suburbs. She'd hardly get to see Angela. They wouldn't be able to afford the expensive bus fares into the city.

She should have kept her big mouth shut this morning. And all over a drop of spilt milk. She'd have to make amends some way. Bridie sighed deeply. Somehow, this time, she felt it was too late.

Chapter Three

Dave Cummins had the shakes. He needed a fix. Badly. His mouth tasted like sandpaper. He felt sick and shaky. He crawled out of bed. He pulled his blue sweater on and stepped into his jeans. His clothes could do with a wash. *He* could do with a wash. He was stinking. But he couldn't care less. He had given up worrying about such things long ago. He used to care about the way he dressed. He'd had a good job in a finance company. But the pressure to bring in more clients was intense.

He'd started taking E at parties. The first time Dave did it, he felt dead guilty. Thinking of his parents and younger brothers in Sligo. Just as well they couldn't see him. They'd be horrified to think that Dave, the pride of the Cummins family, was taking drugs. Gradually

21

the guilt wore away. He started going home less and less at weekends. He was too busy, he told his family. It was important that he socialise and network and make new connections. His family were very impressed and very proud of him.

A friend of his had introduced him to acid and speed. Then . . . cocaine. Before long he'd been snorting lines of the fine white powder like there was no tomorrow. It made him feel good, in control. He felt he could do anything. He moved with a fast set, in the fast lane. He was working all hours. And partying until dawn. He needed the coke to keep going. Only after a while Dave needed more and more of the drug to get his highs. His supplier had offered him heroin. High-grade stuff from Columbia. Dave refused vehemently. No way was he getting involved in heroin. That was a mug's game. You took heroin, you got addicted. You got addicted, you ended up on the streets with nothing. That wasn't going to happen to Hot Shot Cummins.

He'd resisted the pressure for months. But the coke wasn't doing it for him anymore.

He'd been at a party that New Year's Eve in some posh penthouse in Killiney. Drugs and booze flowed freely. He snorted a few lines of coke and waited for it to hit. The rush didn't come the way it used to. He lowered a couple of vodkas and smoked a joint. Stoned, he went into one of the bedrooms and collapsed onto the bed. Only then did he see a pale thin black-haired girl sitting at the dressing-table. She was injecting herself.

"Hi," she mumbled. Dave watched as she sat tense and agitated and then the drug hit her. Her body relaxed. A smile of pleasure crossed her face. All the tension left her. Her lovely face became serene.

"It's the best," she murmured. "The best."

She got up from the chair and weaved her way out of the room.

"Whatever turns you on," Dave muttered and fell asleep.

He often though of that girl and the expression of ecstasy on her face after she had injected herself. The pressure at work was intense. He felt stressed out trying to make his monthly returns target. He was called in by his boss and told he wasn't trying hard enough. His sales performance was considered unsatisfactory. He'd have to try harder. He missed a few payments on his car loan and was threatened with repossession. His girlfriend kept hassling him about getting married. Dave just wanted to forget about the whole damn lot.

He went to a party and got pissed out of his skull. Jeff, his supplier, was there. "Do you want to go on the ultimate trip, Dave?" he invited. "Just do it the once. Believe me nothing else compares."

What the hell, thought Dave groggily. Once couldn't do much harm. And boy was he stressed out. The memory of a pale face with its smile of ecstasy came to him.

That night, Dave took his first hit of heroin. It blew his mind. Jeff was right. It was the ultimate trip. He had never felt such peace and contentment. All his worries evaporated into thin air. Life was better than it had ever been.

Six months later, he was jobless, carless, had no girlfriend and was living in a grotty bedsitter on the North Circular Road. But none of that was important. All that mattered was heroin.

Shivering, Dave pulled on his anorak. He was always cold these days. Still, he'd be all right once he scored. He'd get the money some way. Dave shuffled downstairs and out into the crisp autumn day.

Sara Collins ate her last spoonful of porridge with relish. She finished the rest of her tea and toast. "That was lovely Eddie," she said. She smiled at her husband. He smiled back.

"That will keep you warm, there's a nip in the air today," he said. "Are you sure you don't want me to bring you into town?"

"Certain," Sara said firmly. Today she was going to have a good browse. She didn't want to be put under pressure by her husband. He got impatient if he had to spend longer than two hours in town. She liked to pick things up and look at them and put them down and come back to them again. This drove Eddie mad.

He was a list man. He felt that she should write out a list of what she needed and stick to it. Just like he did. It was good to be organised he told her. It made life easier. It might make life easier but it wasn't half as much fun, was

Sara's view. Besides, today she had a particular reason for going into town on her own. She wanted to buy Eddie's birthday present. She had seen just the thing. A gorgeous miniature grandfather clock. It was so tiny and delicate, hardly much longer than her middle finger. It was perfect for Eddie.

Her husband loved clocks. He'd have them all over the house if she let him. He had a cuckoo clock. A grandfather clock. A Westminster chimes on the mantle that could be heard in Timbuktu. Carriage clocks of various shapes and sizes. Dusting all these clocks got on her nerves. But Sara loved her husband and she put up with his clocks. It could have been worse. It could have been china frogs or elves and gnomes.

He had plenty of room for his clocks, Sara thought as she went upstairs to get ready for her trip into town. The three boys were married with children of their own. The nice four-bedroom house that was the family home was too big for herself and Eddie now. They really should sell up and get a smaller place. But Sara loved her home. It held so many memories.

All her children had been born at home. All the joys and sorrows of their growing up were part of the fabric of the house she and Eddie had lived in since their marriage over fifty years ago. Move! No. They were too old and too settled to face the upheaval of moving house. Moving was for young people. Not the likes of her and Eddie in their mid-seventies.

Sara dabbed some powder on her nose. Then she applied her lipstick. Her hand shook a little. She sighed. Old age was a dreadful thing. Dimming eyesight. Hearing not great. And hands that weren't as steady as they used to be. At heart she felt as young as when she was in her thirties. Ready for anything. Still, she wouldn't dream of going out without her make-up on. Sara had always kept herself smart. Old age wasn't going to change that.

She checked her bag. She needed to get money from the banklink. It was handier than writing a cheque. It was showery but she had her headscarf.

She was looking forward immensely to her day in town. Later, she would treat herself to tea and cakes in Clerys' tea-rooms.

She poked her head around the kitchen door.

"See you later Eddie," she said cheerfully. "There's cold chicken and tomatoes in the fridge for your lunch. I'll get the dinner when I come home."

Her husband waved a sudsy hand. "Don't worry about me. I'll be fine. I'm going to put a bit of compost on the vegetable garden. And I might do a bit of pruning and deadheading."

"Don't overdo it," Sara warned. Eddie was inclined to forget his limitations.

"And don't you spend all our savings," Eddie retorted.

Sara laughed. Eddie was always teasing her about being a spendthrift.

She set off with a jaunty step. The shower was over. The sun shone on the sparkling raindrops trapped in the leaves of the pyracantha. A lovely sight, Sara thought approvingly as she headed towards town.

Chapter Four

Tony walked briskly. It had stopped raining. He was heading north. He decided to walk to Finglas. He was registered at the Fás Centre there. Maybe he might have some luck on the job front today.

The sun came out. It glittered on the waters of the canal as he walked along Cross Guns Bridge. There were nice new apartments built in what had been an old mill. Once he'd believed that he and Jean would have a place of their own. They'd had a deposit saved. Now it was gone.

Tony felt bitter and angry. He'd been a good worker. A person should be able to work if they wanted to. He frowned. Feeling sorry for himself was not going to help. Maybe there'd be something in Fás for him today. At least he was keeping fit by walking, he thought wryly. He was much fitter now than he'd been when he was working.

Fás was on the first floor of the shopping centre. Tony eagerly scanned the boards to see if there was anything new since the last time he'd been in. Surely someone needed an experienced printer. That was what he wanted to do. But he wouldn't turn his nose up at any other type of work. He saw that a porter was required for a city centre hotel. There was no harm in applying, he supposed. The money wasn't as good as he'd been earning, but with tips it wouldn't be too bad.

He went to the girl at the desk. She took down all the relevant details and promised to get in touch with him. There was a lot of interest in the job, she told him. Some of the applicants had hotel work experience already. Tony knew that she told him all this so he wouldn't get his hopes up too high. He'd been through this many times before.

"I'll take my chances," he said.

As he walked out the door of the Fás centre he noticed several people waiting outside in the hallway. They were waiting for the library to open. It was a long time since he'd been in a library, he reflected. When he was a child he used to go to his local library once a week. He'd been a good reader. As he got older and developed interests in sport . . . and girls, he'd neglected his reading. Jean liked reading. She always had her head stuck in a book.

The porter opened the door. The people waiting surged in. Tony found himself following them. It would pass an hour or two. Then he'd have a coffee and a bun and then, he thought dolefully, he'd go home.

He looked around and saw that he was in the bright airy children's section. Little tables and chairs and boxes filled with illustrated story books were in the centre of the area. Larger desks and chairs lined the big floor-to-ceiling window area. Bookshelves crammed with books lined the walls. Posters and paintings were everywhere.

Nice, thought Tony. When Angela was older he'd bring her here and enrol her. He walked along into the next section. The adult library was just as inviting. Easy chairs and small tables were dotted here and there between the bookshelves. There were desks by the windows. A few students were settling down to study. A queue had formed at the lending desk. The staff laughed and chatted with the borrowers. There was a very agreeable friendly atmosphere about the place. Not at all like the intimidating silence of the library of his youth.

He began to browse through the books. He was in the non-fiction section. He picked up a book about painting and decorating and began to flick through it. There were some great ideas in it. He particularly liked one wallpapering tip. It showed a picture of a room with the border strip outlining the door-frame. It looked most effective.

He'd promised Ma Feeny he'd paint and paper her bedroom. Maybe he'd outline the bedroom door with a border. It looked very posh. Ma Feeny would like that. She was into posh. She'd have the neighbours in to show off her new border.

Tony sighed. It wasn't that he didn't like his mother-in-law. She wasn't that bad. He just didn't like living with her. He put the book

down and moved along towards two large racks of cassettes. To think you could borrow tapes as well as books. Tony was most impressed. He saw a Queen tape. Tony loved Freddie Mercury. There was a great selection of tapes. Classical music, pop, spoken arts. There was also a huge selection of Talking Books. It was incredible. Years ago there'd been nothing like that. You went to the library, borrowed your books and that was that.

He noticed a woman returning a large painting. You could borrow paintings as well? This was a right little Aladdin's Cave. Another rack caught his eye. It was full of magazines. *Autocar, Hot Press, In Dublin, Woman's Way, The RTE Guide, Hello!*. There was a great selection to cover all tastes. You could spend all day in the library entertaining yourself, Tony thought as he watched a girl sit down at a computer and a young man who was doing a session in the language lab. There were dozens of languages to learn. Maybe he might start to learn French or German. It would give him something to do while he was unemployed. It would probably cost a fortune to join, Tony thought ruefully. Still, there was no harm in asking.

"There's no charge at all, sir." The affable man behind the desk said.

"Oh!" exclaimed Tony in delight. "Could I join then?"

"Certainly, sir." The librarian smiled and handed Tony a form. "Just fill that out please. Would you have any identification on you? I need some proof of address."

"I have my social welfare card and a letter from the tax inspector. Would that do?"

"That'll be fine, and I'll just check your form against the voter's register."

Just as well he'd filled out the change of address form and sent it in to City Hall when they'd moved in with Mrs Feeny, Tony thought as he wrote his details on the application form.

"When will I get my tickets?" Tony asked.

"You can take out three items today," the librarian said. "You'll get a computerised ticket when you return your books, cassettes or whatever. You can use this ticket in any of the computerised libraries, including the ILAC library.

"That's marvellous!" Tony was delighted. The ILAC was in town, just off Henry Street. He'd always meant to have a look around the very modern library but had never got around to it. "Could you tell me how I'd go about using the language tapes? I'm interested in French."

"You just put your name down for a session. The same if you want to use the computer. You can borrow the course of language cassettes. There's a small waiting list. So I'll reserve it for you." The librarian filled out a little white form and asked Tony for his phone number. "We'll give you a call when part one is available."

Tony left the library with the Queen tape, the decorating book and a Stephen King horror novel. He had put his name down for a session in the language lab and had reserved a copy of *Bravo Two Zero,* the bestselling book about the SAS.

He felt a bit more positive. He hadn't planned to go into the library. But now he was more than glad he'd done it. He had three books to read. God knows he had plenty of time on his hands to get through them. He had his name down to learn French. At least he was doing something positive. He would make the most of this unwanted free time until he got another job, Tony resolved. He would use it to learn.

He went into the coffee shop downstairs. He ordered a cup of coffee and a scone and sat flicking through the decorating book. Jean would find it as interesting as he did. She loved anything to do with decorating. Hopefully by the time he got home her humour would have improved. He'd been a bit hasty himself. He'd apologise. Feeling much more cheerful, Tony finished his coffee and set off for home.

Chapter Five

Jean's heart sank. There was a huge queue in the post office. It was always like that on children's allowance day. Never mind. She'd be richer by forty pounds when she came out. She hadn't collected her last children's allowance. When she could, she let it mount up. Which wasn't very often.

Jean left the post office some twenty-five minutes later with her forty pounds tucked safely down the finger of her glove.

She felt like going on a spree. It was always the same when she got her children's allowance money. There was always the urge to throw caution to the winds and go mad. It was her money to do what she liked with. Tony was always urging her to treat herself with it but Jean would have felt as guilty as hell if she did that.

Angela needed new shoes and vests. She was growing out of her clothes so fast these days. Tony needed new jeans and he could do with a new jacket for the winter. She'd feel extremely mean spending money on herself.

Jean passed the newsagents on her way to the bus stop. She noticed the latest issue of *Hello!* on a display stand. Once, she used to buy it and other magazines regularly. Now they were a luxury she could not afford and she had to make do with furtive reads at the magazine stand. She brushed the thought aside impatiently. Looking back was just being negative. The past was the past. She had to make the most of her situation. There were people much worse off than she was and self-pity got you nowhere.

She was lucky, a bus pulled into the stop just as she reached it and an elderly man helped her with the buggy. Jean smiled and thanked him. Some people could be so nice. Others often barged past and left her struggling.

The traffic was light and it wasn't long before they were in O'Connell Street. The sun had come out again and Jean walked briskly towards the traffic lights enjoying the crisp autumn morning. She liked town. It invigorated her. She stood waiting to cross over towards Henry Street. Now that she was in the city, she was beginning to have second thoughts about traipsing all the way over to the civic offices. If the Housing Department had been in Jervis Street it would have been no trouble.

Jean stood in a tizzy of indecision. Should she go and see about getting a corporation flat or house. She felt a bit guilty. It was like going behind Tony's back. Not that she'd be making a decision there and then, she assured herself. There was no harm in asking.

But she could always phone them, rather than trek all the way across town. That's what she'd do, Jean decided. She'd phone and get all the information and then present it to Tony. They could talk about it then and make a decision together.

The trouble with her, she thought as the lights changed, was that she was too hot tempered. She always had been. She had flown off the handle this morning and got herself all fired up. Typical.

Jean smiled sheepishly. To tell the truth, having thought about it, she wasn't sure if she wanted to move to the outer suburbs. Blanchardstown, Tallaght and Clondalkin and the like were very far out of town. And that was probably where they'd have to go if they were to get a house. Still, if Tony really wanted to get out of her mother's, she'd go. She'd phone the Housing Department and get the information. Then they could talk about it tonight, Jean decided. They could go into the Housing Department together. The main thing was to do it *together*.

Jean felt much more light-hearted as she headed towards Dunnes. Too hell with it, she was going to buy Tony his jeans and the baby her shoes. She was going to treat herself to *Hello!* and she'd buy her mother a bunch of carnations from the flower sellers in Moore Street. It was almost like going on a spree, she thought, with a surge of anticipation. It was a long time since she'd been on one.

Chapter Six

Sara had thoroughly enjoyed her jaunt into town. She had window-shopped and browsed to her heart's content.

The shops hadn't been too crowded. She had picked and poked and compared and contrasted with ease. The joy of it. Eddie would have been driven mad if he'd been with her. Sara patted her handbag. His boxed miniature grandfather clock lay within. She'd gone to Marks & Spencer's food hall and bought him some Florentines, his favourite treat.

She'd enjoyed a cup of coffee and a chocolate eclair in the tranquillity of Clerys' tea-rooms. She liked the tea-rooms. It was a treat being served by a waitress. Sara didn't enjoy these newfangled fast-food restaurants

43

where you had to queue up yourself. If you were going to treat yourself . . . do it properly was her motto.

She sat in the bus on the way home, weary but content. They were almost at Phibsboro. It wouldn't be long now until she was home. She noticed a man cleaning a shopfront window. Tomorrow was her window-cleaner's day. A thought struck her. She had spent more than she intended when she'd got carried away in Roches basement and bought an enormous soft fluffy bath sheet. She'd withdraw some more money from the banklink near the bus stop.

There were two other people in the queue for the banklink. Sara cast an eye at the sky. It had got cloudy again. And cold. She drew her scarf tighter around her. It was going to rain. She hoped it would hold off for five minutes. Just until she got home.

She was glad there was no one else behind her when it was her turn. She was a bit slow sometimes and she didn't like to think she was delaying people. It made her flustered. A minute later a crisp ten pound note slid into her hand.

Grand, thought Sara. She was dying to get home and sit down, put her feet up and let Eddie make her a cup of tea. A spit-spot of rain landed on her nose. If she hurried, she'd make it before the downpour.

Dave Cummins watched the elderly woman queue for the banklink. He was in a bad way. Desperate. He'd gone to meet his dealer hoping to score. He'd promised to pay him the next day, which was Dave's dole day.

The dealer had told him to get lost. No cash . . . no goodies. He shivered. The cold was going right through him. His stomach was cramping something awful. He couldn't concentrate. He had to get some money somehow. He saw the old lady put her money in her bag and walk in his direction. His heart started to race. It would be so easy. She was old, she wouldn't put up much of a struggle. It would be over in a flash. He could disappear down one of the side roads and no one would ever know it was him. He'd never been in trouble. The police wouldn't be looking out for him.

"Just this once because I'm desperate. Just this once," he muttered as he quickened his pace.

Tony couldn't believe his eyes. He watched the old lady struggling with the young man. Then she fell and he was running with her bag.

"Oi! Oi!" he shouted as he raced after him. The bloke turned, looked around and ran faster. But he wasn't fit and Tony was. He caught Dave by the jacket and tried to snatch the old lady's bag. Dave lashed out wildly and caught Tony a glancing blow on the side of the face. Anger surged through Tony.

"You cowardly bastard. Mugging an old lady," he grunted, socking his captive one back. He grabbed the bag as the young man wriggled out of his jacket and tore off. Tony looked at the empty jacket in dismay. He was sorely tempted to go after the thief who'd escaped down a side street. But the old lady was still lying on the ground. At least her bag was safe. He ran back to where she lay.

"Are you all right, pet? I have your bag."

The old lady's face was contorted with pain, blood oozed from her temple. Sara tried to speak but she couldn't.

"Breath slowly, take it easy," Tony said, as he tried not to panic.

A motorist stopped and rushed to help. "I've called the guards and I've called an ambulance." The man knelt down beside Tony to assist him. He had a mobile phone in his hand. Another woman stopped. She wiped the blood from Sara's face.

"You'll be all right, dear," she soothed.

Sara gripped Tony's hand. "Eddie's clock," she whispered. "Eddie's clock."

Tony looked at her, perplexed. He couldn't make out what she was saying.

"What is it?" he asked gently thinking how frail her old hand felt.

"In my bag, Eddie's clock. Is it broken?"

Tony hastily opened the bag and saw what was troubling the old lady. He unwrapped the tissues around the small box, opened it and lifted out the miniature clock.

"It's fine," he assured her just as the ambulance arrived, sirens wailing. It hadn't taken long, but then the Mater Hospital was only minutes away. A look of panic crossed the old lady's face. Her grip tightened on Tony's hand. He thought of his own mother. She was dead now. Imagine if something awful like this had ever happened to her. "I'll come with you," he said. "Don't worry." He saw the relief in her eyes. He'd phone Jean from the hospital if he was delayed. But he couldn't leave the poor unfortunate woman alone. She was clearly terrified.

He sat with her in the ambulance, reassuring her and holding her hand. Her left wrist was broken the ambulance man told him. And he suspected some fractured ribs.

A guard followed the ambulance on his bike. As they followed the stretcher into the accident and emergency unit, he told Tony that he wanted a statement from him.

The nurses were kind to the old lady although it was some time before she was X-rayed. Tony told the guard what had happened and gave as good a description as he could of the mugger. One of the nurses had contacted Sara's eldest son.

"I don't want Eddie to get a fright," she said firmly. Now that she'd got over the shock of it, she was rallying.

"At least the scut didn't get my bag, thanks to you." She smiled weakly at Tony. "You're a decent young man."

"It's time to go for your X-rays," the nurse said.

"What about if Matt comes? What about my shopping?" Sara said agitatedly.

"I'll wait and I'll mind your bags for you," Tony assured her.

"I can't be taking any more of your time," Sara protested.

"I've nothing else to do. Go and get your X-rays taken and don't be worrying," Tony insisted.

"Thanks, son. God will repay you," Sara said feebly. Her ribs and head ached and she wished mightily that she was at home safe and sound with Eddie.

"Matt will be here soon, I'm sure," Tony said giving her hand another little squeeze. He was sorry he hadn't been able to hold on to the gurrier who'd done this to the old lady. He should be behind bars.

It was almost four o'clock. He decided he'd wait for another half hour or so before phoning Jean. He wondered if she was still mad with him.

Soon after a nurse brought a stocky man in his forties over to him. The man held out his hand.

"I believe you've been very good to my mother. I want to thank you. Matt Collins is the name."

Tony shook hands with him. "I'm only sorry I couldn't hang on to the bastard, but at least I got your mother's bag back. She's down having her X-rays."

"Thanks for staying. I'm sure you're anxious to be off. I hope you weren't delayed from work or anything," Matt Collins said, concerned.

"Not a bit of it. I'm unemployed at the moment. My time's my own."

"I'm sorry to hear that." Matt sat down beside him. "What line of business were you in?"

"I was a printer." Tony sighed.

"Go way! I'm in the business myself," Matt exclaimed. "Why did you fold?"

"Ah that postal dispute last year mucked us up good and proper. We never got back on our feet after it. We were only a small firm. The same as many who went to the wall."

"What type of stuff did you do?" Matt asked interestedly.

Tony told him all about the job and the machines he used. They were deeply engrossed in technical detail, and the merits of one machine over another, when a nurse came to tell Matt that his mother's X-rays were completed, her wrist was being set and they were keeping her in overnight for observation. "She'll be fine. We'll let her home tomorrow most likely. We've brought her to a ward and given her a sedative if you want to go up for a few minutes."

"Tell her I send her my best wishes," Tony said as he stood up to leave.

"I certainly will and thanks very much." Matt stood up and shook hands with him. "You'd better give me your name and address. Do you have a phone number? I know Mam will want to say thanks."

"There's no need at all, but I'd like to know

how she is, so maybe she'd give me a call when she's up to it," Tony said as he wrote his name and address on a piece of paper and handed it to the other man.

"Thanks again," Matt called as Tony headed for the exit.

Chapter Seven

"What happened to your face?" Jean exclaimed in horror as Tony walked into the sitting-room.

"It's nothing. An old lady got mugged and I ran after the bloke and got her bag back. He gave me a thump."

"God, Tony you could have been killed!" Jean went pale.

"Don't be daft!" Tony said comfortingly. "Anyway if I had, you'd be a rich woman once the insurance company paid out."

"Oh Tony!" she reproached.

"It was a joke." He held out his arms. "Sorry for losing the cool this morning."

"I'm sorry too." Jean traced her finger gently down the angry red bruise on the side of his face. They kissed, glad the row was over.

"Ma doesn't mean to be fussy, it's just her way," Jean said as they stood together, hugging.

"I know," Tony said. "Listen I joined the library today and I got a lovely decoration book. There's a great idea about doing borders. I was thinking of doing it in her bedroom."

Jean looked at Tony and laughed. "Here was I worrying all day that you might never set foot in the house again, and there's you thinking of ways to decorate her bedroom. I even rang the Housing Department to find out about going on the housing list."

Tony looked at her in amazement. "But you always told me you'd hate to move out to the suburbs."

"I would move if it would stop us having rows. And if it was what you wanted to do," Jean said softly.

Tony's hug tightened. "I love you, Jean, you're the best wife a man could wish for."

"We can go in any time in the morning or afternoon to talk to a housing officer and ask to be put on the housing list." Jean smiled.

"Well, there's no harm putting our names down. I might have a job by then. I went to the

Fás centre today. I'm going for an interview for hotel porter next week. Mind, I'd say there's forty thousand others going as well."

"Don't worry, Tony. We'll manage. You'll get a job in a printers again." She kissed him softly.

"If you young lovers could spare half an hour, your dinner's ready." Bridie Feeny poked her head around the kitchen door. Delicious smells wafted into the sitting-room. She disappeared into the kitchen and they could hear her humming.

Tony raised an eyebrow. "What's going on?"

"I don't know. I was told to go in and put my feet up. She said she was cooking dinner. The fire was lit. So I sat down and read *Hello!* I treated myself."

"You did right," Tony said firmly.

"I bought you a pair of jeans and I got Angela's new shoes out of the children's allowance."

"But that's *your* money," Tony remonstrated.

"It's *our* money, love," Jean responded.

"Dinner," Mrs Feeny warbled.

They walked into the kitchen to find the

table set with the best cutlery. Jean's carnations were arranged in a vase in the centre of the table. There were glasses of wine beside plates of steaming steak and kidney pie, (Tony's favourite). Their mouths watered.

"Sit, sit." Bridie fluttered around pulling out chairs.

"This looks lovely," Tony said.

"Well, we were all a bit tetchy this morning, so I thought I'd do us a special dinner just to show there's no hard feelings on my part," Bridie declared.

"That's very nice of you, Mrs Feeny. And just to show you I've no hard feelings I want to show you a book I got in the library that's got great decorating ideas . . . for when I'm doing your bedroom," laughed Tony.

Bridie's face lit up. "You're going to do my bedroom?"

"Well that's if we don't come to blows over borders and wallpapers and things," teased Tony.

Bridie laughed. "I know I'm a bit pernickety. Don't mind me."

For the first time in ages Jean felt light-hearted. "This is gorgeous, Ma," she said after a mouthful of delicious crisp light pastry.

"Well I know Tony likes it. It was your poor father's favourite," Bridie said. "Eat up, there's plenty more."

They tucked in with gusto and chatted about the day's events. It was the nicest meal they'd had together since coming to live with Bridie. Afterwards they bathed Angela and put her to bed. Then they went downstairs and sat beside the blazing fire and played cards. After such a disastrous start that morning, the day ended on a very happy note. Each of them went to bed that night feeling much more content.

Eddie sat holding Sara's hand. His wife was dozing. He watched her lovingly. Sara was so precious to him. Thank God it was nothing worse than a broken wrist and cracked ribs. The fright he'd got when Matt arrived home and told him what had happened. It was an awful tough world. God be with the days when you could walk the streets and never fear for your safety. There were evil gurriers around for sure, he thought grimly. But then there were nice folk too. The young man that had come to his wife's assistance couldn't have been nicer, Matt said. An unemployed chap. A printer like his son.

Eddie smiled to himself. What goes around, comes around was his motto. Something good would come of that young man's good deed. Matt had plans!

Dave Cummins sat on the cold hard ground. His fingers shook as he positioned the needle. He couldn't even wait until he got home. He had to have it now. It was cold and wet and the alley was dark. He didn't care. He had his fix. He'd robbed two more handbags since his disastrous first effort. Both times he'd been successful and he'd got enough money to buy a couple of hits of his precious heroin. What did he care that he'd terrorised three elderly women. For one very brief moment a wave of self-disgust swept over him as he stuck the needle into his vein. Then it was gone and he felt nothing except relief as the drug took effect and he sat, slumped, in the wind and rain oblivious to the world.

A week later the phone rang and Bridie Feeny answered it. "It's for you, Tony," she called.

Tony picked a piece of wallpaper out of Jean's hair. They were stripping Bridie's bedroom. "Nearly finished," he said encouragingly as she scraped at a particularly difficult piece.

He ran downstairs and picked up the phone. "Hello?"

"Tony. It's Matt Collins. I have a proposition to put to you." Tony's eyes widened as he listened to the man at the other end of the phone. He felt stunned. Shocked. He couldn't believe what he was hearing. A wave of joy enveloped him.

"Tomorrow morning would be fine. I'll see you then and thanks very much, Matt."

"Thank *you*," Matt said firmly before hanging up.

"Jean! Jean!" He raced up the stairs.

"What's wrong?" Jean looked worried as she came to meet him.

"Wrong! Nothing's wrong. Everything's right. Matt Collins has just offered me a job in his printing firm. He owns it, Jean. *He's* the boss and he's asked me to work for him. One of his men is retiring at the end of the month and there'll be a vacancy. I've to go in and see him tomorrow." The words were tumbling out of him.

"Tony. Oh Tony," Jean squealed in delight as her husband lifted her in the air.

"I knew something would come up. I just knew it," Tony exclaimed. "Our luck's going to change and all because I helped an old lady. Who'd believe it."

"This is the third happiest day of my life," Jean declared giddily.

"What were the other two?" Tony asked, grinning.

"The second was the day Angela was born. The happiest day was the day I married you."

"Mine too." Tony smothered her in kisses as they hugged and danced around Bridie's bedroom amidst the piles of stripped floral wallpaper.

"It's better than winning the Lotto. I can't wait to get back working again. We'll get our house sometime. We'll buy one near your Ma. We'll go on a holiday. We'll do all the things

we planned we'd do. We're on the way up again." Tony brandished his scraper. "Let's get to it. I want to have this room done before I start work. Jean, I feel ready for anything. It will be good practice for when we get our own house."

Thrilled with themselves, they set to with a will that not even the most stubborn patch could resist.